Immigrants bound for America aboard the
SS *Westernland*, circa 1890, NPS

Ferry landing at Ellis Island, circa 1900, NPS

ELLIS ISLAND

Gateway to the New World

LEONARD EVERETT FISHER

Holiday House / New York

Ellis Island, NPS

Immigrants arriving in New York Harbor,
circa 1900, THE BETTMANN ARCHIVE

America fever!

"You just had America fever, and that was all there was to it," said Hulda Carlson. Swedish-born Hulda came to the United States in 1910, a girl of sixteen.

The "fever" rose as the ships carrying immigrants to the United States at the end of the nineteenth and the beginning of the twentieth century neared the American coast. The passengers had spent some three weeks crossing the often stormy Atlantic Ocean. They jammed the rails waiting to catch their first glimpse of America, whatever the season, whatever the weather, seasick or not. Few spoke, lost as they were in the reality of their arrival. Soon the distant flat and sandy landscape of Rockaway Point and Coney Island could be seen rising out of a bluish haze on the right. To the left were the low, rolling hills of New Jersey and Staten Island silhouetted against the western sky. As the land closed in and the gray green water of Lower New York Bay lapped at the rolling ships, Norton's Point Lighthouse and Brooklyn loomed on the right, seeming close enough to touch. On the left Swinburne and Hoffman islands appeared to brush the ships' sides. Three or four miles dead ahead was the Narrows, the entrance to New York Harbor, a mile-wide neck of water guarded by Brooklyn's Fort Hamilton and Staten Island's Fort Wadsworth. The weary immigrants fell silent with excitement and expectation.

As each ship slowly sailed through the Narrows into Upper New York Bay, it veered slightly north-northeast toward Manhattan, toward the West Side piers on the Hudson River. The river seemed to stretch wide and endlessly ahead. The crowded buildings of Lower Manhattan rose from the low land like stony spectators in a fairy tale. Everywhere the immigrants looked, the harbor was packed with ships of every size, from every nation around the world. They were coming or going, at anchor or tucked into the enormous piers that poked the rippling tides like monstrous fingers. From the huge British four-stack Cunard White Star liner *Mauretania* to the small Russian-American Line steamship *Korea,* most of these ships carried thousands upon thousands of immigrants among their passengers. These hopeful strangers to a new land, pressing the ships' rails, could only gasp at the busy scene.

Quickly, their scanning eyes caught the one object they had waited a lifetime to see. It was the symbol that said more about why they had come to America than anything else on earth. Off the port bow, at the center of the fast-moving harbor activity, was the vision of their dreams, the Statue of Liberty. Called *Liberty Enlightening the World,* the statue had been a gift to the people of the United States from the people of France. The work of French sculptor Frédéric-Auguste Bartholdi (1834–1904), it became a harbor fixture on October 28, 1886, the day it was dedicated. Some cheered. Some fell to their knees and prayed. Others wept. They had arrived. The dream had come true. A half-mile beyond the statue, closer to the Jersey City docks than to Manhattan, was Ellis Island, their "Gateway to the New World." Here, at Ellis Island, their fate would be decided. After being examined and questioned, they would either be admitted to the United States or be sent back to where they had come from. The immigrants fell silent again—this time with worry and dread. Would they become Americans or would they be sent back?

The fever to leave the Old World for America from 1892 through 1954—the sixty-two-year period of Ellis Island—seared the souls of approximately fifteen million people. While many thousands of immigrants entered the United States during this time at various ports—Boston, Philadelphia, Galveston, San Francisco, and others—these fifteen million arrived in New York

The Statue of Liberty, NPS

City and were processed at the Ellis Island Immigration Station. In 1907, a record number of 1,285,349 immigrants were admitted to the United States. Of these, 1,004,756 were processed at Ellis Island. Although immigration was not a new event in the American experience—French, Germans, Poles, Irish, Danes, and Swedes; Russian, Spanish, and Portuguese Jews; Chinese contract laborers, and the English Pilgrims were all earlier immigrants to America—these fifteen million represented the largest movement of human beings in history.

They came from everywhere in Europe, but chiefly from eastern and southern Europe. There were exceptions. In 1911, small numbers of black women from French possessions in the West Indies had begun to trickle into Ellis Island. Still, the greatest surge of people to reach American shores originated in Europe between 1892 and 1914. And most of them came because they were hungry, poor, and without a future. They came because they were unwanted or unrewarded. They came to think and say what they believed without fear. They came for adventure, too. But mostly they came for opportunity. And they came first to Ellis Island.

Long before white people had ever heard of the North American continent or sailed into New York Harbor, Ellis Island was little more than a three-acre sandbar. There, roosting sea gulls squawked and oysters thrived, providing food for the local mainland Indians. The Indians had always called this near-desolate place Gull Island or Oyster Island. They sold it to the Dutch West India Company in 1634 for little more than a trunkful of trinkets. The Dutch West India Company had been colonizing New Amsterdam, a tiny settlement at the tip of Manhattan Island, since 1613. The company in turn sold the barren island to one of the New Amsterdam colonists, Mynheer Paauw. By the time the

Immigrants from Guadalupe, French West Indies,
April 6, 1911, NPS

Dutch surrendered New Amsterdam to the British in 1664—the British renamed the settlement New York—Mynheer Paauw owned much of the present-day New Jersey shoreline along the Hudson River facing Lower Manhattan. His heirs continued to own chunks of New Jersey real estate under British colonial rule, selling off bits and pieces over the years, including Gull or Oyster Island. For a short time during the 1700s the island was nicknamed Gibbet Island. The British had erected a gibbet, or gallows, on it for hanging criminals, most of whom were pirates. Finally, Samuel Ellis, a colonial merchant, bought the sandbar during America's War for Independence (1775–1783). The Ellis family kept the island until 1808, when they sold it to New York State.

New York State turned the island over to the federal government. The government needed to build a fort on the island. In fact, the government needed to build a number of forts in and around Upper New York Bay to protect New York City against a growing threat of British naval activity in the area.

Great Britain, at war with France, was stopping American ships that were trading with Europe, especially those trading with France. English marines were boarding unarmed American merchant ships, removing American sailors, and putting them on English ships to fight in England's war. On June 27, 1807, the British sailed into New York Harbor and attacked the American frigate *Chesapeake*. The Americans fought back by firing the guns of Fort Jay and Fort Columbus on Governor's Island, but with little success. The attack put the United States on a collision course with England once more—the soon-to-be-fought War of 1812.

Quickly, between 1808 and 1811, the federal government built a number of forts in the upper New York Harbor area: Fort Wood on Bedloe's Island, renamed Liberty Island in 1956, the future home of the Statue of Liberty; Castle Williams on Governor's Island; the Southwest Battery—an island fort 200 feet off the tip of Manhattan; the North Battery farther up Manhattan's West Side; and Fort Gibson on Ellis Island. None of these military stations influenced the outcome of the War of 1812. Only two of them would remain until today: the forts on Governor's Island, which continued as a military post, and the Southwest Battery, now a historic landmark called Castle Clinton.

Fort Gibson on Ellis Island would disappear without ever firing a shot. Some of Fort Wood on Bedloe's Island would become part of the foundations of the Statue of Liberty pedestal. The North Battery would fade away. But the Southwest Battery, connected to Manhattan by a shaky wood drawbridge, would eventually be linked with Ellis Island's history after pursuing an extraordinary destiny of its own.

In 1815, following the end of the War of 1812, the Southwest Battery was renamed Castle Clinton after DeWitt Clinton (1769–1828). He had been a presidential candidate, a senator

DeWitt Clinton, LEONARD EVERETT FISHER

Jenny Lind, circa 1850,
COURTESY OF THE NEW YORK HISTORICAL
SOCIETY, NEW YORK CITY

from New York, mayor of New York City, and, later, governor of New York. Castle Clinton was the headquarters of the Third Military District of New York for six years. The roofless, round brick island fortress was abandoned in 1821 when the headquarters were moved across the water to Governor's Island. In 1823, however, the federal government gave Castle Clinton to New York City for whatever purpose the city might find useful. A year later, during the summer of 1824, Castle Clinton, renamed Castle Garden, opened as a center for fashionable entertainments. The officers' quarters were turned into a bar.

This was the spot where the important, the famous, the infamous, and the near-famous came to see and to be seen. And usually they came by boat. Here the Marquis de Lafayette (1757–1834), an aging French aristocrat who fought the British at the side of George Washington (1732–1799), landed to begin a final and celebrated tour of America. Here, too, came presidents and politicians of every stripe to accept the applause and praise of other public officials. By 1850, Castle Garden had a roof and had become a very popular theater and opera house. Jenny Lind (1820–1887), the singer dubbed the Swedish Nightingale, made a sensational American debut here. By now, Castle Garden was no longer an island but was joined to Manhattan by landfill.

Not long after Jenny Lind's concert, Castle Garden was closed. The city of New York had leased it to the state of New York to be used as a reception center for immigrants. Since the 1840s, immigration into the United States had increased noticeably. But between 1848 and 1854, ships laden with immigrants chiefly from Ireland, Germany, and France overloaded the docks of New York Harbor. It had become difficult to have an orderly immigration process and to protect the immigrants from thieves and thugs. These criminals waylaid the newcomers as they stepped from the docks into the street traffic, robbing them and sometimes mur-

Castle Garden, circa 1880,

COURTESY OF THE NEW YORK HISTORICAL SOCIETY, NEW YORK CITY

dering them as well. This midcentury wave of immigrants was the result of political unrest and poor harvests in Europe, and the failure of the potato crop in Ireland. Since immigration was a function of the individual states rather than the federal government, the state of New York decided that Castle Garden was the best place to process and protect the immigrants.

Castle Garden opened August 3, 1855, as the New York State Immigration Station. Immigrants could receive medical attention if they needed it after their long, hard voyage. The weary travelers could also change their money for American money, make arrangements for journeys to other places in the United States, and obtain information about housing. All this was supposed to take place without anyone having to worry about the crooks along the docks. In due time, plenty of shady people worked their way into the seemingly safe Castle Garden Immigration Station and cheated the bewildered immigrants there as well.

Castle Garden opened just in time as an immigration station because the numbers of immigrants began to swell beyond anyone's expectations. Beginning in 1882–1883, the immigrants from northern and western Europe were joined by those from eastern and southern Europe. The migration continued to grow to such a degree that the event was called the New Immigration. Many of these recent immigrants were Jews fleeing the organized massacres, or "pogroms," of eastern Europe following the murder of Alexander II (1818–1881), the Russian czar. Many more were Italians from the south of Italy, Greeks, Austro-Hungarians, and Poles. So great was this human traffic that the United States Congress decided that immigration control had to be a function of the federal government and not of the individual states. The immigration process passed from the state of New York (and all other states) to the United States government.

The firm hand of the federal government was immediately established. In 1882, the Congress passed a law preventing certain types of individuals and particular groups of individuals from entering the United States. Convicts, so-called "insane" people, and those who had no skills or obvious means of support were not permitted entry. Also among those denied entry were the Chinese and, later, the Japanese. American labor complained that Asiatic people worked for wages too far below those of the average American wage earner. In addition, their customs and living standards were unacceptable to Americans. The complaints were so loud, especially in the western part of the United States where

Hungarian immigrants, circa 1910, NPS

most Chinese and other Asiatics entered the country and lived, that they resulted in a series of rulings between 1882 and 1902 called the Oriental Exclusion Acts. These acts prevented thousands of Asians from entering the United States.

By the time Castle Garden outgrew its usefulness and closed—on April 18, 1890, after thirty-five years of operation (1855–1890)—about twelve million people had emigrated to the United States from around the world. Some 8,500,000 of these came to New York and passed through Castle Garden. The work of Castle Garden would now be taken up at a newer and roomier immigration station, Ellis Island. But it would take two years and a half-million dollars to complete a complex of new buildings. Meanwhile, the immigrants kept coming in even greater numbers and were temporarily processed at Castle Garden's Barge Office. On December 10, 1896, six years after it had closed as an immigration station, Castle Garden had become an aquarium. Called the Aquarium, it remained one of the world's greatest places to see nearly every living species of fish until 1941. On August 12, 1946, the historic building that had been Southwest Battery, Castle Clinton, Castle Garden, and the Aquarium was declared a national monument. It was restored to its early appearance and was once again called Castle Clinton. The entire area is still known to New Yorkers, however, as the Battery.

When Ellis Island opened its doors on Saturday, January 1, 1892, to the first immigrant—Annie Moore of Cork, Ireland—the site, now expanded to twenty-seven acres and protected by a seawall, had docks and a number of wood buildings of different sizes. The largest of these was a two-story, 400-by-150-foot building that loomed over the island landscape. This great structure had storage places for baggage on the first floor and examining areas on the second. Included, too, in the upper story were banks where

The Barge Office, circa 1890,
COURTESY OF THE NEW YORK HISTORICAL SOCIETY, NEW YORK CITY

A Russian Jewish immigrant, circa 1895, NPS

immigrants could exchange their money for American money, railroad ticket counters where they could buy tickets to anywhere in America, snack bars for the hungry, and offices. The other, smaller buildings held a hospital, a laundry, a bathhouse, a kitchen, a dining hall, quarters for doctors and nurses, a dormitory for immigrants who had to stay overnight, and a power plant. In and around these wood buildings were the brick remains of old Fort Gibson. Both the United States Army and Navy had made use of Ellis Island in the nineteenth century. The army had operated Fort Gibson until the end of the Civil War, mostly as a training ground for recruits. The navy used Ellis Island as a storage area for arms and ammunition between 1835 and 1890. The old powder magazines—the bins used to store ammunition—were cleaned out long before any immigrants set foot on Ellis Island.

None of the new buildings was anywhere near completion when Annie Moore stepped off the Ellis Island ferry. Construction continued for five years as thousands upon thousands of hopeful immigrants passed through the new depot. Finally, the Ellis Island Immigration Station was completed on June 13–14, 1897. During the early morning hours of June 15, the entire installation burned to the ground. All the buildings on the island were smoldering ruins by daybreak. The cause of the fire has remained a mystery. Luckily, no one was hurt. But all the immigation records beginning in 1855 were lost. Transferred from Castle Garden, the records were stored in the abandoned United States Navy powder magazines. The heat of the fire reduced all of the records to ashes. The loss of the papers was a terrible catastrophe not only for the federal government but for millions of immigrants. Their record of legal entry could not be readily established.

Ellis Island would have to be rebuilt. And it was useless to try to examine thousands of immigrants on the island in makeshift sheds while rebuilding. The entire process was removed once

The Ellis Island fire, June 15, 1897, LEONARD EVERETT FISHER

25

more to the temporary depot at the Battery's Barge Office. For the next three years, 1897 to 1900, immigrants were pushed and hurried through the entry process at the Barge Office. By December 1900, although still incomplete and costing the considerable sum of a million and a half dollars, the new buildings of the Federal Immigration Station on Ellis Island were ready to receive immigrants. On the 17th of that month the first voyagers to be processed were 2,251 immigrants—chiefly Italian—from four different vessels.

Immigrants leaving their ship for Ellis Island processing, circa 1897, NPS

Many of the immigrants had no idea that they would be examined to see if they were fit enough to be Americans. They thought the ship would just pull up at a New York pier and they would get off. This was true for those immigrants who had the look of the upper class—money, elegant clothes and jewelry, fancy luggage, an educated manner, and a fine, comfortable shipboard cabin. These people simply answered a few polite questions, if any at all, and walked down the gangplank. For the vast majority who crossed the ocean by steerage class—the lowest, meanest, and cheapest way to sail across any ocean—this was not quite the case. Crowded like cattle in damp, smelly holds, they were shocked to learn that they would be kept aboard ship until the better-class

Immigrants arriving at Ellis Island
for processing, circa 1897, NPS

immigrant passengers disembarked. Later, they were herded aboard ferries and taken to Ellis Island, where, if all was in order, they were allowed to board ferries for Manhattan.

At times Ellis Island was so crowded and docks were so few that hundreds of immigrants were kept aboard the ships, riding anchor for days in the waters around Lower Manhattan. Packed aboard these ships in the most unhealthy environments imaginable, they were no longer certain that life in America would be better than the miserable lives they had left behind.

United States Immigration Service ferry
with Battery Park in the background, NPS

". . . and when we came here, we couldn't get off in the same day. We had to wait three days because there were so many immigrants to get off the boats. We had to wait on the boat," remembered eighty-eight-year-old Concetta Rossi.

Concetta Rossi was sixteen years old when she left Reggio Calabria, Italy, in 1907. Shortly afterward, in 1908, an earthquake devastated the area, killing her mother, among others. Concetta Rossi was so seasick aboard the SS *Lacarujack* that she hardly remembered the trip. Yet those three days aboard ship in New York Harbor were forever etched in her memory. When she finally left the ship and passed through the Ellis Island routine, New York was celebrating the Fourth of July.

Nineteen years old in 1923, Kathleen O'Brien, a native of Ballinasloe, Ireland, took three different ships and more than two weeks to get into the United States. Her experience was similar to that of Concetta Rossi.

"We came on a ship called the *Leviathan* . . . we were transferred there [at Cherbourg, France] to the *Isle de France* . . . we arrived in New York after about two weeks . . . so then we transferred to another ship . . . the *Polk,* and then we were left there . . . for quite a few days . . . in the ship. And we didn't know if we were allowed to get off or not. We were there quite a while when we got the word that we were going to Ellis Island."

The immigrants' first good look at Ellis Island came on the ferryboats that transferred them from the ships they arrived in, now snug in their berths at Manhattan piers. The island itself seemed hardly higher than the waterline. The buildings appeared to rise out of the water like an imaginary city in a storybook. Behind them were the docks of Jersey City. The main building, with its ornate towers, red brick, and busy appearance, stood out more

Ellis Island landing area, circa 1910,

31

like a palace than what Kathleen O'Brien described as the place where "they put you through the mill."

Once off the ferry with bag and baggage, the immigrants lined up under a large canopy at the main entrance. From this point and with the help of interpreters—few immigrants outside of the British Isles could speak English well, if at all—they slowly shuffled toward the doors behind which their futures waited. Inside the main building they deposited their belongings on the cavernous first floor. Many would never see them again, for they were stolen by shifty island workers, some of whom had been immigrants themselves. Immediately, their ears were assaulted by the echoing and hollow din of talk, laughter, tears, sobs, and screams all melting together. It was a noise so constant that it bounced around and above them like a wavy sigh. The noise followed them up the grand staircase and into the fifty-six-foot-high balconied second floor of the Great Hall. Here, confused and uncertain, they were prodded and pushed into a maze of aisles formed by iron pipe bars.

Their single-file climb up those stairs was observed by uniformed United States public health doctors to the left and right of them. Those who wheezed, who seemed weak or mentally unsound, who were blind or crippled, and who otherwise had a difficult time climbing the stairs were quickly marked with a piece of colored chalk. There was a different mark for each problem—X for mental disorders, K for hernia, SC for scalp disease, H for heart. Those so marked were separated from the crowd for a physical examination. Immigrants with heart problems, eye infections, scalp diseases, tuberculosis, and other, incurable diseases were placed in the hospital or locked in a cage. There they were held for as long as it took to put them on a ship and send them back to where they had come from. Men, women, and children who were deaf and dumb or mentally handicapped regardless of the reasons

Immigrants under canopied main entrance to
Ellis Island processing center, circa 1900, NPS

The Great Hall, circa 1910,
WILLIAM WILLIAMS PAPERS, THE NEW YORK PUBLIC LIBRARY

were locked up as well and sent back to their homelands.

The chalk mark had tragic, heartbreaking results for untold numbers of families. The Sopirovs of Krolevitz, a small town in the Chernigov province of southern Russia—mother, father, and eight children (three additional children were already in America)—saw an *X* placed on their four-year-old daughter, Natasha, a deaf mute. The child was separated from her parents, brother, and sisters as a "mental defective." The family had to make an on-the-spot decision. Either they would all go back to a place from which they had been driven and where in all likelihood they would be killed; or only the child would go back to live with relatives in a safe place until the family could bring her to America. The family decided that they could not return and that four-year-old Natasha had to go back without them. It would be temporary, they reasoned. A compassionate United States could never be so cruel as to permit such a family separation permanently. Accompanied by an older sister, the child went back to Russia. The rest of the family was admitted without incident but with much anguish, in October 1906. The older daughter was admitted a year later after seeing her small sister settled with relatives. The separation became permanent. The Sopirovs pleaded with the United States government for their daughter's return, with no results. They never saw Natasha again.

Often, immigration doctors would board a ship before it docked just beyond the Narrows. Here they would quickly go through the passengers, looking for signs of serious illnesses. People thought to have such illnesses were taken off the ship right then and there and placed in the Ellis Island hospital. The most deadly cases—persons suspected of typhoid fever or smallpox, for example—were sometimes brought to Hoffman Island in the Lower Bay area. The rest of the passengers were kept aboard ship in quarantine. The ship was not permitted to dock for as many

Immigrant men undergoing physical examination, NPS

days as it took to make sure that the disease would not be brought into the country. This could have been a possible reason why Concetta Rossi spent three days aboard the SS *Lacarujack* riding at anchor in the harbor. The ship could have been quarantined.

Fiorello Henry La Guardia (1882–1947), a son of immigrants who would one day be a mayor of New York City (1933–1945), did much to ease the hardship and disappointment of those who were found too sick or handicapped upon arrival to be admitted to the United States. As an American consular officer in Fiume, Italy, in 1906, he persuaded the United States Department of State to have as many immigrants examined at their ports of departure—before they came to America—as was possible.

For most, however, the experience of admittance was quick and trouble-free. Aristotle Pappas tells what it was like for a youth of eighteen. He had come from a small town in Greece aboard the Austro-American Line ship SS *Getty*.

Mayor Fiorello H. La Guardia, MUSEUM OF THE CITY OF NEW YORK

Immigrant women undergoing physical examination, NPS

"When I came off the boat they took me to Ellis Island . . . They examine me there, my eyes. As soon as they found out my eyes were okay, they let me off."

The eye examination was the most uncomfortable and most feared of all the examinations an immigrant had to face. A medical officer would insert a hooklike instrument, usually an ordinary buttonhook, under the upper eyelid. He would fold the lid over to expose the upper part of the eyeball. The discomfort was downright painful. The doctor was looking for any sign of trachoma, a very contagious eye disease that often resulted in blindness. Immigrants discovered to have trachoma were not admitted to the United States. If the immigrant had healthy eyes before arrival at Ellis Island, he or she could have developed an eye disease after leaving the place because the conditions were so unsanitary. The doctors rarely changed the buttonhook tool and only dunked it in a dish of alcohol to clean it after each use. Worse still, these doctors never washed their hands between examinations. They simply wiped them on a towel usually hanging on a pipe railing.

"We were really bewildered by the process itself and, of course, we were in the company of a lot of people who were in a similar position," said Commander Sigmund Schweitzer of the United States Merchant Marine Academy, King's Point, Long Island. Born in Poland in 1910, he had emigrated to the United States with his parents from Austria in 1921.

The tenseness of "Will I make it?" or "Will I be sent back?" gripped all the immigrants as they worked their way through the ironbound aisles to face the uniformed examiners. Above them on the balcony American spectators watched the endless, anxious parade of immigrant men, women, and children, sometimes

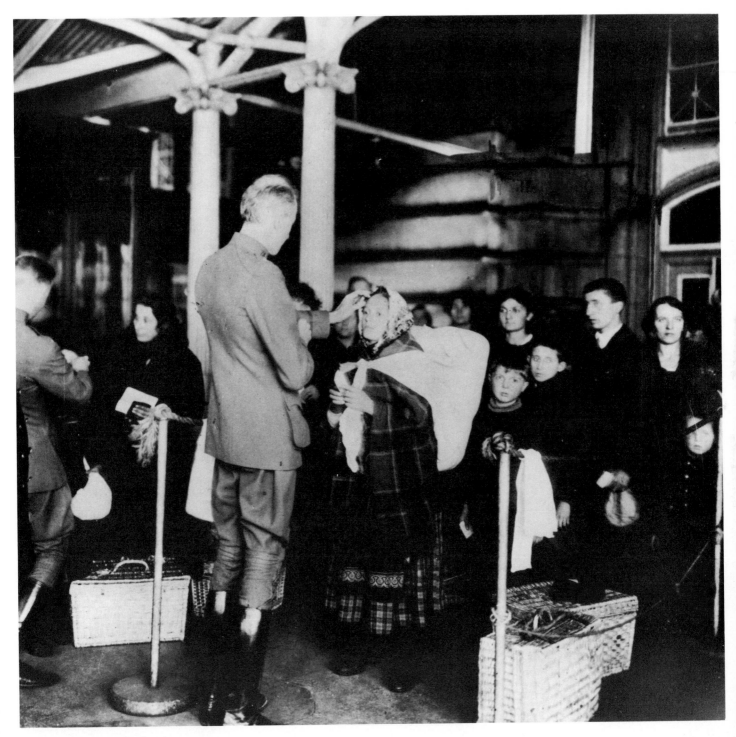

The eye examination, NPS

41

alone, sometimes with entire families, moving closer, ever so much closer to becoming Americans. And to remind each and every immigrant of what he or she hoped to gain, a large American flag hung from the wall ahead of them.

"When we arrived in Ellis Island everyone was very nervous," related Leah Chernofsky Perlman. Mrs. Perlman came from Bialystock, czarist Russia, in 1916, a young lady of sixteen. "We passed through the lines and there were men on either side, and on some of the people those men put chalk marks on their back. Of course, the people themselves did not know it, but the people in back of them could see it and were worried and wondering what it was all about. Only later we learned that those men noticed something unusual, either physical or something else, and they wanted to examine those people more thoroughly."

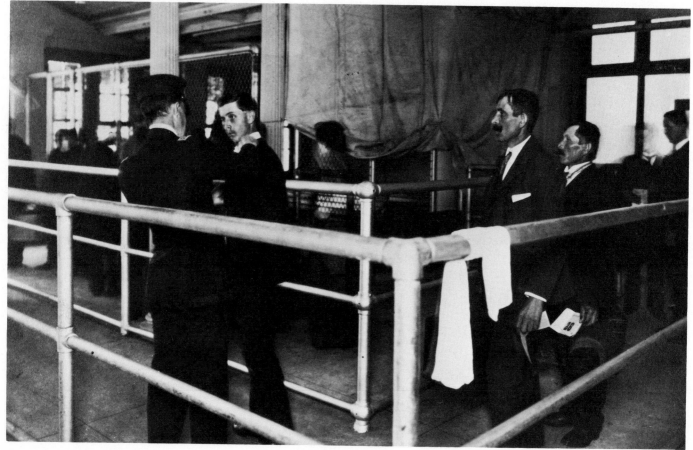

Immigrants being inspected for noticeable physical defects, NPS

The chalk mark, LEONARD EVERETT FISHER

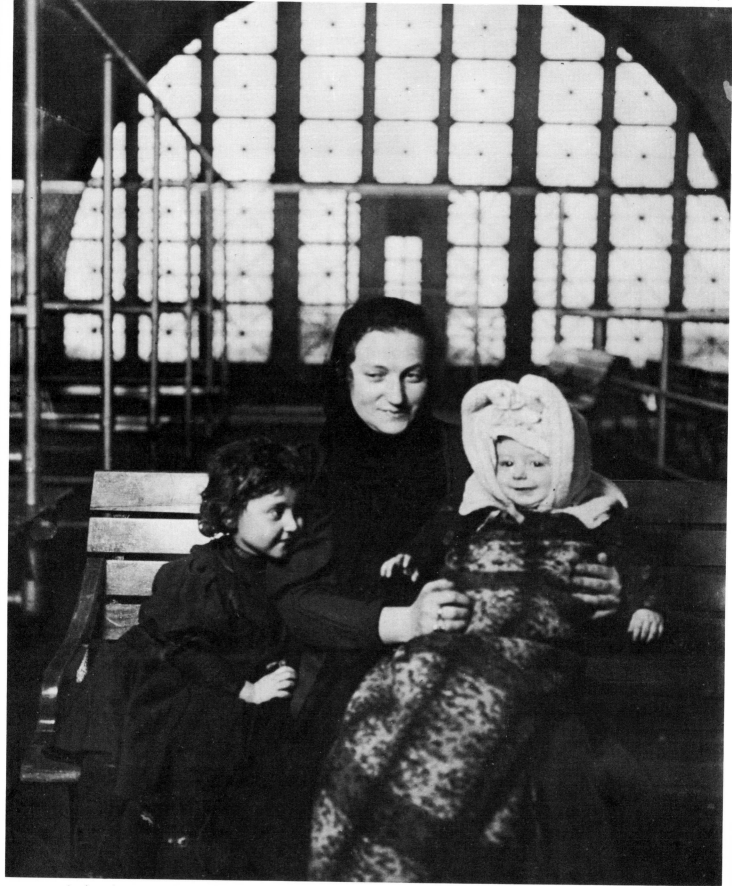

44   An immigrant mother and her
      children await questioning, NPS

Once past the medical inspectors, and if not singled out for further examination by a chalk mark, the immigrants were made to sit on wood benches along with other passengers from their ship. The group moved foward from bench to bench until, one by one, each individual was called before an inspector for questioning. The inspector along with an interpreter was positioned at the end of a railed aisle.

"What is your name? Can you read and write? Are you married? Where is your wife? Do you have children? Where are they? Have you ever been in jail? Have you ever been sick? How do you feel now? How did you earn a living in the old country? How will you earn a living in America? Do you have a job waiting for you? Is someone meeting you? Who? How much money do you have? May I see it?" And more. Often these physical and oral examinations could not be completed within the workday hours. In those instances, the immigrants were held overnight in dormitories and fed at the expense of the American government.

Inspectors questioning an immigrant, NPS

Immigrant children dining in Ellis Island mess hall, NPS

Immigrants viewing Manhattan from the
Ellis Island rooftop playground, NPS

Once the examinations were completed, the immigrant was given a landing card—the permit to enter the United States. Now he or she was free to board a ferry for Manhattan or to purchase train tickets for destinations outside of New York. In the latter case, the immigrant was usually shuttled over to New Jersey rail depots.

Of the fifteen million people who came to Ellis Island between 1892 and 1954, some 200,000 to 300,000 were not admitted for various reasons. However, approximately seventy-nine out of every eighty immigrants were admitted. Or, to put it another way, about 99 percent of all those seeking admission were admitted. These figures do not include those resident aliens who for one reason or another—usually the commission of a crime—were sent to Ellis Island to be deported to the country of their origin.

Little by little, however, pressure was mounting to limit the

NPS

Immigrants passed for entry into the United States, NPS

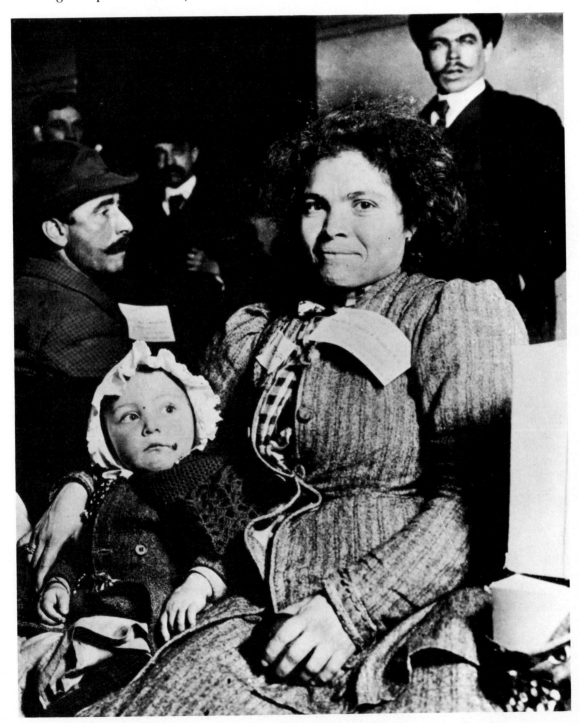

numbers of non-Oriental immigrants applying for admission. In 1891, Congress passed an act that added "people without funds"—paupers—to the Exclusion Acts then in force. Polygamists (people married to more than one person) and people whose boat tickets were bought by someone other than their relatives were excluded as well. In 1903, during the administration of President Theodore Roosevelt (1858–1919), people of "low moral tendency" or of "unsavory reputation" or who were "believers in anarchistic principles"—in other words, all those who might be a threat to the government—were denied admission. In addition, there were congressional acts of 1897, 1913, and 1915 that required immigrants to be able to read and write in their own language. In each instance these acts were vetoed, by Presidents Grover Cleveland (1837–1908), William Howard Taft (1857–1930), and Woodrow Wilson (1856–1924).

In 1909, William Williams, the New York State Commissioner of Immigration, interpreted the federal laws on his own. He decided that each adult immigrant had to have the same as twenty-five United States dollars on his or her person before admission. The law said that adult immigrants, once admitted to the United States, had to be able to take care of themselves and their children, that they could not depend on the government to support them. But the law did not say how much money the immigrants needed to prove that they could take care of themselves. Only Commissioner Williams decided. He and the American public (which now included millions of former immigrants) wanted to slow down or stop altogether the tidal wave of immigration from southern and eastern Europe, chiefly from Italy, Greece, and southern Russia. Again, they wanted to keep out cheap labor. Cheap labor posed a threat to American wage earners.

A great cry went up both in the United States and in Europe. Twenty-five dollars was a considerable sum of money at the time.

Immigrant children in the main floor baggage room, circa 1910, NPS

Newly arrived immigrants at the main entrance
to the Great Hall, circa 1900, NPS

Few immigrants could save any money beyond their boat fare, which averaged thirty to forty dollars one way by steerage class from a northern European port. And the fare was often paid for by relatives already in the United States. More unfortunates were turned back by Commissioner Williams's rule while he was in office (1909–c. 1914) than at any other time in the history of Ellis Island. The twenty-five dollar requirement endured. So did the immigrants. They kept coming by the thousands.

The federal government also decided to tighten up on the number of immigrants entering the country. It denied entry to all those who were generally not in good health, did not have a trade, and did not have enough money to keep themselves from becoming public charges. Ellis Island had become a focal point in the gradual shutting off of free-flowing immigration to America. And much of this would occur after World War I (1914–1918).

Immigration slowed down considerably during the early years of World War I. People could not move easily across the European battle zones to ports. And the ports themselves were too crowded with wartime business to deal with immigrants. Many would-be immigrant men—French, German, Austro-Hungarian, Russian, British, Italian, Serbian, Croatian—were being drafted into their countries' armies to fight. In addition to all this, the seas between Europe and the United States were alive with submarines and surface naval vessels, making any trip across the Atlantic a dangerous adventure.

When the United States finally entered the war in 1917, there was no immigration activity at Ellis Island. Instead, Ellis Island was used as a prison for German sailors caught in American, British, and French ports—Allied ports—at the outbreak of the war. More than two thousand of them were held in the dormitories and first-floor baggage room of the main building.

However, the United States prepared for what it knew would

Italian immigrant men aboard the
SS *Fried de Grosse,* circa 1910, NPS

be a new wave of immigration once the war ended. In 1917, the Congress finally passed a law requiring that all immigrants sixteen years of age or older be able to read and write in one language in order to be admitted to the United States.

Following the end of the war, ships packed with immigrants began to arrive in New York Harbor once again. But this time the hopeful immigrants found themselves unable to move through the immigration steps as quickly as in prewar years. Whereas it had taken only a few minutes to pass unchalked people through the various admission steps before the war, it now took much longer. The literacy test added more time to the process. As a result, not only was it more difficult to be admitted, but there was a never-ending traffic jam on Ellis Island. Constant delays caused an increase in the number of immigrants kept overnight. Dormitories became overcrowded and dirty. The cages where problem immigrants were held became overcrowded, too. The dining halls, overwhelmed by the hordes, were messy. The food served was nearly inedible. The mountain of baggage left on the first floor, although never safe in the best of years, was now regularly picked over by thieves among the island's labor force and among the immigrants themselves. The immigration officers, medical workers, and staff who were directly responsible for the examination and admission of the immigrants and the administration of the island had become overworked, short-tempered, and rude. Still, to many who came to America, Ellis Island was a near-paradise compared with the level of existence they had left behind. Indeed, America if it were free of the immigration processing, would be Paradise itself to them.

During the three postwar years, 1919 to 1921, Ellis Island had become a nearly unmanageable operation. By 1921, however, the United States had no further need for skilled European labor. Thanks to more than a half-century of practically unrestricted

European immigration, Old World skills were deeply rooted in American crafts, industry, and labor. The United States did what it could to discourage Europeans from coming to the United States and entering American industry. Now the majority of those seeking admission to the United States were examined by immigration and State Department officials at the country of their origin—before coming across the ocean. This system greatly relieved the overworked Ellis Island staff and restored a better-controlled process. Immigrants were still examined at Ellis Island, but only as a quick routine follow-up to the "point of origin" examination. Special cases were still set aside at Ellis Island for closer study.

Between 1921 and 1929, the flow of immigrants was severely restricted by a series of quota laws. The Immigration Act of 1924 fixed the number of immigrants of a single nationality—other than Orientals—who could enter the country at 2 percent of its population in America as it was in 1890. If there were 200,000 Danes in America in 1890, then only 4,000 Danes could enter the country in a single year. In addition, the Immigration Act of 1924 limited the total number of immigrants who could enter the United States in any given year to 150,000. By 1929, the quota requirement had not changed much. But Congress added a different twist to an immigrant's application. By passing the National

Immigrant baggage, LEONARD EVERETT FISHER

Origins Act of 1929, Congress said that no matter from what country an immigrant was seeking admission, that person would be counted in the quota set for his or her country of birth. For example, a Dane who was applying for admission to the United States from Norway would be placed in the quota set for Denmark.

By 1931, the number of immigrants entering the country was almost zero. The Ellis Island Immigration Station had become a nearly noiseless place. Missing were the great crowds of immigrants who passed through the entry process of former years. The intense activity that marked Ellis Island in the years 1892–1914, before the outbreak of World War I, had ended. Clearly, Ellis Island was a fading institution. The deportation of unwanted persons was more common than the admission of acceptable immigrants.

By 1932, the Immigration and Naturalization Service, operat-

ing under the United States Department of Justice, had closed down the immigration process at Ellis Island. For the next eight or nine years the island was used as a place to imprison those who were being deported rather than to welcome those who were being admitted. In 1932 alone, some 20,000 persons were deported from Ellis Island. A year later, in 1933, as the Great Depression made huge sections of the American population jobless and nearly homeless, more than 125,000 people left the United States for their native lands, where things seemed to look better. In that year only 26,000 people entered the country.

Still, between 1933 and 1941, about 250,000 refugees from Hitler's Germany and other European areas of turmoil and war entered the United States through Ellis Island. Many of these were European intellectuals and included such people as the physicist Albert Einstein (1879–1955), and the writer Thomas Mann (1875–1955).

When the United States entered World War II in 1941, Ellis Island became a Coast Guard station. At the end of the war in 1945, Ellis Island became a reception depot for more than 300,000 persons who, because of the war, were without a country and had no place to go. These special immigrants were permitted entry by an act of Congress, so they were not subject to the quota system, which had begun in 1921 and which continues to operate under the McCarran-Walter Act of 1952.

By 1954, there was was not a single immigrant or deportee on Ellis Island. The Immigration and Naturalization Service had moved to Lower Manhattan. The federal government wanted to sell the island and its thirty-five buildings to anyone who would commercially develop the property. No one was interested. In 1956, Ellis Island was declared a national park. Twenty-nine years later, in 1985, its restoration as a historic site neared completion.

Dr. Albert Einstein, INSTITUTE FOR ADVANCED
STUDY, PRINCETON, NEW JERSEY

Ellis Island today remains a haunting reminder to the eternal echo and hollow din of the millions who passed through to become Americans—to the talk, laughter, tears, sobs, and screams all melting together like a wavy sigh. And Ellis Island will stand in New York Harbor as a historic reminder of who most of us are—the children of immigrants from every nation in the world, and of every race and creed.

Immigrants of different nationalities, NPS

The Great Hall, circa 1918, NPS

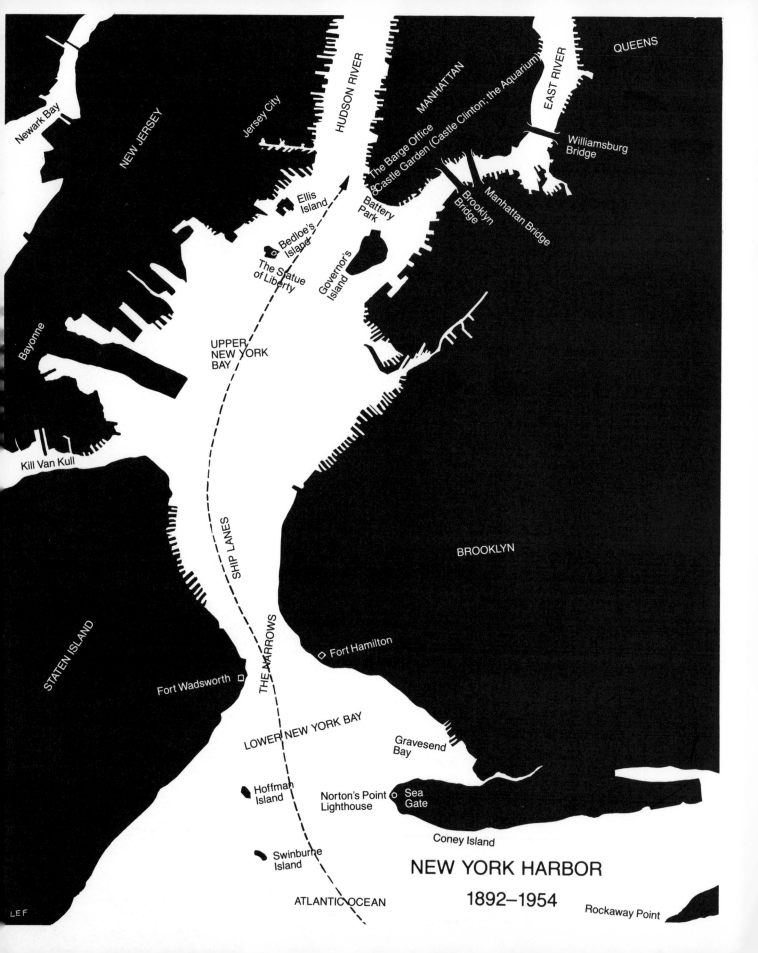

NEWARK BAY

NEW JERSEY

Jersey City

HUDSON RIVER

MANHATTAN

The Barge Office
& Castle Garden (Castle Clinton; the Aquarium)

EAST RIVER

QUEENS

Williamsburg
Bridge

Ellis
Island

Battery
Park

Brooklyn
Bridge

Manhattan Bridge

Bedloe's
Island

The Statue
of Liberty

Governor's
Island

Bayonne

UPPER
NEW YORK
BAY

Kill Van Kull

BROOKLYN

SHIP LANES

STATEN ISLAND

Fort Hamilton

Fort Wadsworth

THE NARROWS

LOWER NEW YORK BAY

Gravesend
Bay

Hoffman
Island

Norton's Point
Lighthouse

Sea
Gate

Coney Island

Swinburne
Island

NEW YORK HARBOR

1892–1954

ATLANTIC OCEAN

Rockaway Point

LEF

Index

(Italicized numbers indicate pages with photos.)

Ellis Island as seen from an approaching ferry, NPS

AUTHOR'S NOTE

The names of most of the immigrants appearing in this book are pseudonyms of actual people. Their identities have been hidden to protect their privacy. Their words were taken from transcribed accounts on file in the Library of the American Museum of Immigration on Liberty Island, New York Harbor. Annie Moore, Albert Einstein, and Thomas Mann are not pseudonyms.

I wish to thank Mr. Won H. Kim, Librarian of the American Museum of Immigration, Liberty Island, New York Harbor, for his patient assistance. The credit line NPS by many of the photographs in this book is an abbreviation for National Park Service: Statue of Liberty, N.M./American Museum of Immigration.

And in remembrance of things past: My mother, Ray Mera Shapiro Fisher, passed through Ellis Island on October 26, 1906, as a child of six. "Someone gave me a banana to eat," she recalled. "I had never seen one before. And that is all I can remember of that day other than my sisters and a cousin meeting us and taking us to Brooklyn."

Library of Congress Cataloging-in-Publication Data

Fisher, Leonard Everett.
Ellis Island.

Includes index.
SUMMARY: A history of immigration through the port of
New York, with special focus on the processing at
Ellis Island.
1. Ellis Island Immigration Station (New York,
N.Y.)—History—Juvenile literature. 2. United States
—Emigration and immigration—History—Juvenile
literature. [1. Ellis Island Immigration Station
(New York, N.Y.)—History. 2. United States—Emigration
and immigration—History] I. Title.
JV6483.F57 1986 325'.1'0973 86-2286
ISBN 0-8234-0612-1

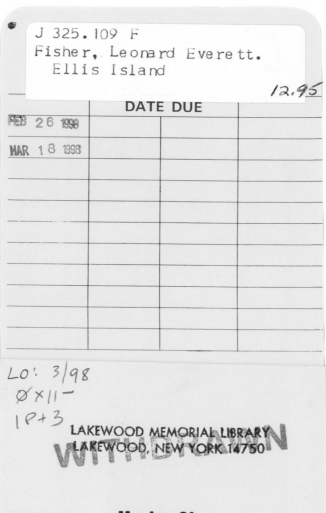